Dinosaurs on the Beach

AN
ORCA
YOUNG
READER

Dinosaurs on the Beach

Marilyn Helmer

ORCA BOOK PUBLISHERS

National Library of Canada Cataloguing in Publication Data

Helmer, Marilyn

Dinosaurs on the beach / Marilyn Helmer.

"An Orca young reader"

ISBN 1-55143-260-9

1. Paleontology--Juvenile fiction. I. Title.

PS8565.E4594D56 2003   jC813'.54   C2002-911457-8

PZ7.H37565Di 2003

Library of Congress Control Number: 2002116172

Summary: Josie is sure that she has found tiny dinosaur footprints in stone, hundreds of millions of years old, but will she be able to secure her find?

Orca Book Publishers gratefully acknowledges the support of its publishing programs provided by the following agencies: the Department of Canadian Heritage, the Canada Council for the Arts and the British Columbia Arts Council.

Cover design: Christine Toller • Cover illustration: Ljuba Levstek

Interior illustrations: Cindy Ghent • Printed and bound in Canada

CANADA	UNITED STATES
Orca Book Publishers	Orca Book Publishers
1030 North Park Street	PO Box 468
Victoria, BC Canada	Custer, WA USA
V8T 1C6	98240-0468

05 04 03 • 5 4 3 2 1

To puzzle-solvers everywhere who will search until they find that missing piece.

Acknowledgment

Thank you to my son, Christopher, for reading the manuscript and using his background in geology and paleontology to offer helpful comments. Thank you also to Tina Smith in Parrsboro, Jeff Day at *The Hamilton Spectator* and the Research Department at Hamilton Central Library for answering my numerous questions.

Josie's Promise

Claire popped her head into the front seat between Josie and Grandpa. "Hey, Josie, what are you reading?" she asked. Josie held up her book.

"*The Secret of Lost Island*," Claire read aloud, snapping her gum. "That's a good one."

Ethan leaned forward, baseball cap jammed down over spiky red hair that matched his twin's. "Here's what happens ..."

"Don't tell me," Josie ordered, blocking her ears.

Claire gave her brother a poke. "Don't

spoil it for her, Ethan. Come on. The game isn't over yet. It's your turn." The twins disappeared into the backseat and dice rattled.

Josie reread the page she'd been reading when Claire interrupted. She closed the book with a sigh. Even her favorite author, B.J. Byers, couldn't hold her attention today.

Grandpa caught her mood. He burst out singing, "If you're happy and you know it clap your hands ..." Josie joined in and they ended with a loud, "Shout hurray!"

"Hurray for the weekend!" said Josie.

"Hurray for spring break!" Ethan added.

"Hurray for Grandpa and me!" Josie cheered. "We get to spend a whole week at Stone Trees Cottage by ourselves. We'll go fossil hunting and beachcombing every single day."

"Best hurray of all is for Ethan and me," Claire spoke up. "We get to go to Montreal with Mom and Dad." She gave Josie's braid a tug and snapped her gum again. "Too bad you're not coming."

"Little One, she can't come," Ethan singsonged.

Josie turned and glared at her brother. "I could've come if I'd wanted to," she said. "But I'd rather stay with Grandpa. And quit calling me Little One."

"Ethan, don't tease," said Grandpa.

"Dr. Larsen calls her Little One all the time," said Ethan. "How come you never tell him to stop teasing?"

"I don't think Bill says it to tease," Grandpa replied.

Someday I'm going to give Dr. Larsen a piece of my mind for sticking me with that nickname, Josie told herself. Aloud she said, "You thought *little* was pretty neat when you found that fossil bone last year."

"Our best find ever," said Ethan, not even trying to hide the pride in his voice.

"Whoooee!" Grandpa exclaimed. "I'll never forget that day."

"We were fossil hunting," Claire jumped in. "Dr. Larsen was with us, remember?"

"It was just past Fiddlehead Cove," Ethan said.

"By the big rocks," Josie added.

"I picked up a stone and there was a little bone in it," Ethan went on.

Claire laughed. "You yelled so loud, you scared up a whole flock of gulls."

Josie glanced at Grandpa. "You said, 'That bone's so tiny it must have come from a really little creature.'" She'd never seen Grandpa so excited.

Grandpa grinned at Ethan in the rear view mirror. "I knew for sure you'd made a great find, Ethan. That bone had to have come from a dinosaur smaller than any we'd recorded to date."

"Remember how excited Dr. Larsen was?" Claire spoke up. "And he's a paleontologist. But he said we had to find more proof."

"Hey, we're in the middle of a game," Ethan reminded Claire. "It's your turn. Hurry up and roll the dice."

The twins returned to their game, but Josie's thoughts stayed on the little bone. "What kind of proof?" she'd asked Dr. Larsen.

"Something that will show us just how little the creature was," Dr. Larsen had said. "Like a skeleton, even part of a skeleton. Or the eggshell the creature was born in. Or footprints." He'd gone on to explain. "Paleontology's like a jigsaw puzzle. You look for the pieces and fit them together. If you find the right puzzle pieces, you end up with a picture of the creature and proof that it existed."

Josie had made herself a promise that day. A promise she hadn't told anyone, not even Grandpa. I'm going to find the proof Dr. Larsen is talking about, she had told herself. I like doing jigsaw puzzles. And I love looking for things, especially secret, hidden things. Yes! I, Josie Renee McCrimmon, am going to find the pieces of that dinosaur puzzle.

She made a mental list. She had already found some pieces. More bits of bone. One that looked like the tip of a tail. A curved piece that might be part of a jaw. But not enough to complete the puzzle. Not enough to prove that such a little dinosaur existed. Not yet.

Squirming restlessly, Josie looked

out the window. "There's no fog today."

"The tide's in now," said Grandpa, "but it will soon be on its way out, so we'll have plenty of beach to explore. After lunch we'll be hitting the best time of the day."

"There have been lots of storms lately," Josie said. "Maybe new slabs and chunks of rock will have broken away from the cliffs. New secrets waiting to be found." She glanced at Grandpa, willing him to drive faster.

Grandpa caught her look. "We're almost there," he said, turning the van onto Old Beach Road.

"Look!" Josie exclaimed. "Someone's fixed up the Fergusons' cottage."

Claire popped up. "They painted it my favorite color," she said. "Neat, eh?"

Josie stared at the sky-blue walls and white trim. The bright colors looked out of place among the sand, rocks and wild grass. She liked the narrow two-story cottage much better the way it had been, weathered to a ghostly gray.

Suddenly there was a movement on the porch and something hurtled down the steps toward them.

"Watch out, we're going to hit him!" Ethan shouted.

Grandpa braked as a large white dog raced at the van. Teeth flashing, it jumped against the door in a barking frenzy.

Josie screamed and went rigid in her seat. A hand gripped her shoulder. "It's okay, Jo-girl," said Grandpa.

"You're safe, Josie, he's outside," Claire said.

A boy ran around the side of the cottage, waving his arms and shouting. The dog raced back to him.

Josie rubbed her sweaty palms on her jeans. "The Fergusons never had a dog before," she said, hoping her voice wasn't shaking as much as her insides were.

"The Fergusons sold the cottage," Grandpa said. "I met the new owner, Jim Dunham, the other day. The dog belongs to his nephew, Lucan." He glanced at Josie. "Lucan's just visiting for a few days, so the dog won't be around long."

Josie chewed at her lip. "He's awfully big," she said. "And he sounds mean."

Grandpa put his hand over hers. "I'll speak to Jim and make sure Lucan keeps that dog under control," he promised. "By the way," he went on, "Jim owns a store in Halifax called The Rockhound."

"We've been there," Ethan said. "Remember? It was just before Christmas."

"We bought that amethyst paperweight for Aunt Virginia," said Claire.

"I remember," said Josie. Half the store was a museum. It reminded her of Stone Trees Cottage, filled with rocks and fossils of all kinds. The shop itself had many interesting things for sale. But the prices — whoooee!

"So, McCrimmons, we won't be the only fossil hunters on the beach," Grandpa said. "We'll have some pretty stiff competition from Jim and Lucan."

Josie stared at Grandpa. "What do you mean?"

"Most of the rocks and fossils in

Jim's shop are ones he found himself. Now he has Lucan helping him. Lucan had made a couple of good finds the day I met them."

Josie sucked in her breath. "What?" Oh, please, not *little* bones, not *little* eggshells.

"A couple of plant fossils," said Grandpa, "and some petrified wood."

Josie let out her breath in a relieved whoosh. "We'd better get out there before he finds something really important."

"I'll bet this Lucan kid doesn't know all the stuff we know about dinosaurs," Claire said.

"Right," said Ethan. "Like that dinosaurs lived here centuries ago. Maybe they even walked right where we're driving now."

Claire looked out the window. "Way back when it was all lakes and rivers and plants and trees."

Josie, too, looked out at the windswept shore. "That's all gone now," she said. "But we know what it was like from the fossils we've found." Her eyes searched the beach. Somewhere out there are the puzzle pieces of that little dinosaur, she told herself. Someday, someone is going to find those pieces and put them together. And that someone is going to be me.

Stone Trees Cottage

As they rounded a bend, Josie whooped, "There's the cottage!"

It was her favorite place in the whole world. Grandpa's cottage, the last one on Old Beach Road, sitting high on a grassy rise overlooking the ocean. The paint on its faded walls was peeling, leaving patches of weathered gray wood. Beyond, the broad strip of land between the road and shore narrowed. Stone cliffs rose in the distance, curving out of sight.

"Who wants to go fossil hunting?" Grandpa asked.

"I do!" Josie and Ethan spoke almost together.

"Me too," said Claire. "Hey, let's have a bonfire on the beach tonight."

"We can barbecue hot dogs." Ethan smacked his lips. "And toast marshmallows."

Claire added her own lip-smacking sounds. "Can we? Please? Toasted marshmallows are the best thing in the world."

Grandpa chuckled. "You must have read my mind. I brought hot dogs and marshmallows too, so we're all set."

"Mom sent potato salad," said Ethan.

"Dad packed us a lunch," said Claire. "Chicken sandwiches and chocolate chip cookies."

Grandpa swung the van into the driveway. "My stomach's rumbling already," he said. He turned to Ethan and Claire. "How about you two collect some driftwood? Jo-girl can help me bring the stuff into the cottage."

The minute the van stopped, Josie yanked the door open and hopped out. Ethan and Claire scrambled after her.

"Last one to the beach is a rotten fish!" Ethan yelled. He raced off, neck and neck with Claire.

"We'll be there in two shakes of a billy goat's tail," Josie called after them.

Neither Claire nor Ethan looked back. Josie didn't care. She was with Grandpa in the best place in the world. She closed her eyes and drew in a deep breath. "Sea air smells better than a flower garden," she said.

"For sure," said Grandpa. "Better than autumn leaves burning."

"Better than ..." Josie thought hard, "Dad's world-famous spaghetti sauce."

"Nothing can out-smell that," said Grandpa. He swung his old duffle bag onto his shoulders and picked up a box of groceries. Josie grabbed her suitcase and a small cooler and followed him up the steps.

Inside, she put the cooler on the kitchen counter and took the suitcase to the bedroom she shared with Claire. On her way back through the living room she stopped and looked around, pretending that she was seeing the cottage for the first time.

From the outside, Stone Trees Cottage looked like any of the dozen or so summer houses that dotted the coast along Old Beach Road. Inside it was different. Everywhere you looked, Stone Trees Cottage was filled with secrets from a time long past.

Oddly shaped rocks, petrified wood, sharks' teeth and polished stones crowded the shelves and windowsills. The broad wooden mantle was covered with fossilized bones and stone footprints of creatures that had lived thousands of years ago.

"Bill Larsen dropped by the other day," Grandpa said as Josie came back into the kitchen. On the table sat a familiar-looking box.

He had a note in his hand. "Bill says thanks for lending him the fossils. He says the school classes he visited got a kick out of seeing fossils that other kids had found."

Josie glanced at the note. Frowning, she pushed a loose clump of hair behind her ear. "He called me Little One again," she said. "I'll bet he thinks I'm too young to be a paleontologist like he is."

Grandpa reached into the box and picked up a gray stone. A fragment of curved bone stood out against the dark surface. On the back was a sticker with Josie's name on it. "It doesn't matter whether you're big or little ..." Grandpa waited for Josie to continue.

"Sharp eyes and a keen mind are what counts," Josie finished with a grin. "I found that one near where Ethan found the little bone."

"It's a good find, Jo-girl," said Grandpa.

"You bet," Josie declared. "Good enough to put in my record book." She went over to a large cabinet, opened a door and took out a pile of notebooks.

There were four books, one for each of them. Grandpa's was on top, a thick leather-bound book with a gold crest in the middle. Josie knew without looking that the book was more than half full.

She ran her fingers over the grainy cover. Oh, to have a book like this one. The record books were special. Only their very best finds were listed.

Beneath Grandpa's book was a ratty,

tatty green one. Claire had printed "FOSSIL FINDS" across the front. Below were all their names, but Ethan's and Claire's had been crossed out. Only Josie's remained.

The cover of the book was faded and the corners were creased and curled. Josie grimaced. The book was a mess. It was water-stained too, because she'd once dropped it into a tidal pool.

Ethan's book was next, new and neat, with pictures of fossils on the cover. Josie opened it. Seventeen entries filled the first page. The eighteenth was on the next page, all by itself. It was the little bone, the one Grandpa and Dr. Larsen were so excited about. Ethan had drawn a picture of it. Josie stared. If that bone could talk, what secrets could it tell them?

Under Ethan's book was Claire's, with eleven entries including part of an ancient eggshell, plant fossils and a shark's tooth. It was like Ethan's book except that it had sparkly fish and shells all over the cover.

Claire and Ethan had found the books

at the mall last year. They had each copied their finds from the green notebook into their fancy new ones.

"I'll rip out our pages so the old book will be just yours," Claire had said. So Josie was left with a note-book that was falling apart, a note-book no one else wanted.

"Let's get these groceries put away, Jo-girl." Grandpa's voice tugged Josie's thoughts back to the present. She put the notebooks on the table.

"Better not forget the potato salad," said Grandpa, reaching for the cooler. As he put the lid aside, it bumped the stack of record books. Josie's ratty, tatty green one fell to the floor. She picked it up and put it back on the table.

"Know what, Grandpa?" Josie stood on tiptoe to put bread and buns into the cupboard. "Someday I'm going to have my very own record book. It's going to be the best one ever. It will have pages and pages and pages of all the ..." she searched her mind for the right word "... fabulous things I find!" She closed the cupboard door with a whack. "Let's go!"

"In a minute, Jo-girl." Grandpa filled the kettle and set it on the stove. "It's a chilly day so we'll need some tea and hot chocolate to warm us up."

Josie got the thermoses. While they waited for the kettle to boil, Grandpa thumbed through the notebooks. When he came to Josie's he said, "I think you're due for a new one."

Josie shook her head. "I'm going to wait until I have something really, really great to write about," she said. Like puzzle pieces. Little puzzle pieces of a little dinosaur.

The kettle whistled and Grandpa busied himself making the tea and hot chocolate. Josie opened the ratty, tatty green book. Five entries. A piece of petrified wood. Everyone had found some of that. A clam shell and part of a plant. And the curved bone fragment and the tiny tail tip.

The last two were Josie's best finds so far. Good ones. Puzzle pieces. But not the kind of proof Dr. Larsen was talking about.

Josie closed the book and dropped

it on the table. "Grandpa, I want to find something special," she said. "Something wonderfully, amazingly, super special. Something ..." She stopped and clamped her lips together. That something was still her secret.

Grandpa grinned. "How's that going to happen?"

"Hard work!" Josie replied, grinning back at him.

"You betcha!" said Grandpa. "Eyes open, mind alert and leave no stone unturned."

Josie gaped at him. "There must be a gazillion stones on the beach!"

"So we have our work cut out for us, don't we?" said Grandpa.

Josie grabbed the picnic lunch. "We're never going to find anything hanging around here," she said. "Come on, Grandpa. Let's go fossil hunting!"

A Nasty Encounter

"We found lots of wood already," Ethan shouted when he saw Josie and Grandpa coming. He and Claire were dragging a huge piece of driftwood across the pebbly sand toward what looked like a small fort.

"I saved some neat pieces for Mom," said Claire, "for her sculptures."

"We'll make sure we don't put those on the fire," said Grandpa. He looked at the big pile. "But we'll still have a bonfire that'll light the beach for miles tonight."

Claire rubbed her stomach. "We'll

roast a million hot dogs."

"Don't forget the marshmallows." Ethan smacked his lips.

"Speaking of eating," said Grandpa, "how about lunch?"

Josie opened the bag and everyone dug in.

Overhead the sun still peeked through, but gray puffball clouds were closing in, growing thicker and heavier. Josie gulped her sandwich and drink, eager to get going before rain ruined the hunt.

When they were finished, Ethan collected everyone's garbage in the bag and shoved it between two rocks. "We'll get it on the way back," he said. "Come on, let's go."

Grandpa pushed himself to his feet. "We're off," he said, shrugging his backpack onto his shoulders.

Ethan took the lead. "Let's walk up to Old Stone Trees."

Josie looked into the distance. From where she was standing, she could only see as far as Stone Trees Point. There, the jagged cliffs jutted out, blocking from view what lay beyond. Fossilized tree stumps stood upright along the cliff's face like a line of soldiers. It was known as Old Stone Trees and that's where Grandpa's cottage had gotten its name.

Josie's heart beat faster. Rounding the point was like opening a surprise package. You never knew what you were going to find on the broad rocky beach beyond. She moved ahead of the others, hoping to speed them up.

"It's the best time of year for fossil hunting," said Grandpa, keeping pace. "Too early in the season for tourists and too cold for beachcombers."

"Except us." Ethan picked up a flat stone. "The winter storms have been helping us again."

"And the tides," Claire added. "They help too, tearing away chunks and layers of rock."

"Showing us secrets," Josie said in a spooky voice. "Secrets that have been buried here for a long, long time. You never know what you're going to find."

"Maybe you'll find a whole dinosaur,"

Ethan teased with a grin. "Maybe a whole live dinosaur. Wouldn't that be something, Little One?"

Josie's temper flared. "Don't call me that, Ethan McCrimmon. I hate that name."

"Little One, she's no fun," Ethan singsonged.

"Ethan." Grandpa's voice was firm. "Enough."

Ethan quit teasing, but his grin stayed put. He dropped the stone he'd picked up a moment ago and stooped to examine a larger one. When he caught Josie's eye behind Grandpa's back, he pretended he was a dinosaur stalking along the beach.

Josie ignored him. They were almost at Stone Trees Point. "We're the only ones on the whole beach," she said, turning to face the others.

"No, we aren't," Claire said. "Someone else is coming."

Josie turned back. A tall bearded man had just rounded Stone Trees Point. He saw them and waved.

"It's Jim Dunham," said Grandpa.

"Hey, Jim," he called out. "Great day for beachcombing."

"Uh, oh!" Josie heard the warning in Ethan's voice. "There's that dog we saw this morning."

Josie stopped, heart thumping. Rounding the point was the boy she'd seen at the blue-and-white cottage. He was dressed in a bright red jacket and hiking boots. At his side was the large white dog with a stick in its mouth. The dog dropped the stick and the boy picked it up and hurled it. "Fetch, Hunter!" he yelled. The stick landed right at Josie's feet. As the dog bounded toward it, Josie screamed and scrambled out of the way.

Grandpa grabbed the dog's collar and held it back. Jim raced forward and took control. "Sit, Hunter!" he ordered the wriggling dog. To Josie he said, "He won't hurt you. He's just a puppy."

The dog half sat, barking and whining. Josie backed away. Could anything that size be just a puppy?

"Lucan's teaching Hunter to fetch," Jim said. "Better put his leash back on," he added as his nephew caught up with them.

Lucan gave his uncle a sulky look, but to Josie's relief he did as he was told.

"Neat dog," said Ethan, approaching Hunter. Hunter jumped at him, almost knocking him over. But when Ethan patted Hunter's head, the dog's hind end wagged with pleasure. He trotted over to Claire, then to Grandpa, yelping and whining for attention. As he turned toward Josie, she backed farther away.

Lucan gave her a mocking grin. "Are you scared of dogs?" He made it sound as though he were asking if she was afraid of butterflies. He moved toward her, bringing Hunter closer. Josie scrambled away and Grandpa said firmly, "Please hold that dog back."

Lucan scowled, but he did stop. Hunter pulled at his leash while Josie watched him warily. When Lucan saw her discomfort, his scowl became a smirk.

"We'll keep Hunter on a leash from now on," Jim said.

"We'd appreciate that," said Grandpa, and they went on to talk about the fossil cliffs.

Lucan turned his attention to Ethan and Claire. "Your grandpa told me that you've found some neat fossils around here," he said. "My uncle's going to pay me for any good stuff I find."

As he talked on, Josie studied him silently. He was taller than Ethan and husky, with a broad face and straight brown hair. His eyes were dark. They reminded Josie of wet pebbles.

"Maybe we can go fossil hunting together," he suggested.

"Claire and I are going to Montreal on Monday so we won't be around," Ethan said. "But Josie'll be here all week."

Lucan looked at Josie with a disinterested shrug. That didn't bother her. She had no interest in fossil hunting with Lucan.

"Speaking of fossils," Jim said, "I was talking to Bill Larsen the other day. He told me about a tiny bone one of you found last year. Asked if I'd ever come across anything like that. Did you find the bone around here?"

"I'm the one who found it," Ethan jumped in. "Just past Fiddlehead Cove, near the big rocks."

"Fiddlehead Cove?" Lucan was all ears. "Where's that?"

Before Ethan could answer, Grandpa interrupted. "Bill mentioned that he'd been to your shop," he said to Jim. "He told me you've got quite a collection yourself."

"Fossils are a passion of mine," said Jim. "Tourists and collectors come from all over to visit my museum. In the summer I can hardly keep my shop stocked." He turned to Ethan. "I'd like to have a look at that little bone," he said. "I might be interested in buying it from you."

"Really?" said Ethan. "Josie found some little bones too." Josie's attention was on Lucan, watching as he let Hunter's leash out longer and longer. But when she heard her name, she tuned back in. "Just pieces, not a whole one like mine," she heard Ethan say. "We figure the bones must have come from a really little dinosaur so we're look-ing ..."

Josie could hardly believe her ears. Ethan was about to spill out the secret place! She cut him off with, "Sky's getting darker. It's going to rain soon."

"You're right, Jo-girl," said Grandpa. "If we're going to do any beachcombing today, we'd better get a move on." He nodded at Jim and Lucan. "We'll be seeing you."

"That's for sure," Jim replied.

But Lucan wasn't quite ready to move on yet. "Little dinosaur bones, eh?" he said. "I'll bet stuff like that is worth a lot of money." He patted Hunter. "I need to make some big bucks so's I can pay for him."

"Pay for Hunter?" Ethan asked.

"Yeah." Lucan straightened up. "Uncle Jim loaned me the money to buy Hunter. I have to pay him back. Bones like that little one you found would be worth a few bucks." He looked right at Josie, the smirk back on his face. "So you'll be seeing a lot of me around here. And Hunter too," he added. With a tug on the leash, Lucan walked away, leaving Josie staring after him.

As soon as he was out of hearing, she whirled on Ethan. "Why did you have to tell him about the little bones?" she huffed. "Now he's going to be looking for them too."

Ethan frowned. "I didn't think about that," he said. "I should have kept my mouth shut."

"No use crying over spilled milk," Grandpa said. "Let's get on with our fossil hunting before the rain ruins our plans."

Grandpa, Claire and Ethan moved ahead, but something on the ground caught Josie's eye. It looked like a giant black beetle. She bent to examine it. "Mermaid's Purse," she said, picking up the hollow egg sack that had once held a baby skate fish. She put it into her backpack. It would be something interesting to bring to school for the science display.

A shout from behind caught her attention. Lucan was watching her. "So where's Fiddlehead Cove?" he called out.

Josie shrugged. "That's my secret," she called back.

Lucan began walking toward her. As Josie moved away, a sly smile crossed his face. "I'm real good at finding out secrets," he said. Hunter strained at his leash. "And Hunter's real good at helping me."

Josie turned and hurried after the others. Lucan's mocking laugh followed her. A sick feeling settled in the pit of her stomach. Just how good was Lucan at finding out secrets? And what did Hunter do to help him?

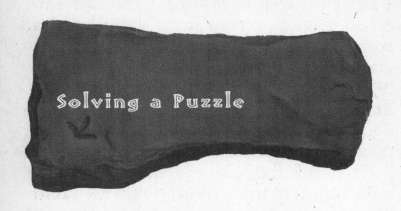

Solving a Puzzle

"Fiddlehead Cove dead ahead," Claire announced as they rounded Stone Trees Point. Grandpa's cottage was no longer in sight.

From where they were standing, Josie could see the edge of the gap where the sea washed in. Grandpa once told them how, long ago, the cove had started as a split in the rocks. Over centuries, tide and waves had carved it wider and deeper, like a sculptor carves a statue. The cove was narrow and well protected by the high cliff walls. As they headed toward it, Josie, Claire and Grandpa stopped here and there to examine things that caught their attention.

Ethan, impatient, went ahead. Suddenly they heard him shout. "Hey, come here, you guys! Look what I found!"

Josie and Claire raced to catch up. When they rounded the edge of the cove, Ethan was examining an old fishing boat that had run aground on the rocks. "I wonder whose it is," he said.

Josie and Claire clambered over the side. While Claire picked her way cautiously among the debris that littered the bottom of the boat, Josie searched for any secrets it held. She spotted a dark shape under the seat. Dropping to her knees, she pulled it out.

"What have you got there, Jo-girl?" Grandpa asked, joining them.

"It's just an old sweater," Ethan butted in with a snort of disgust. And that's what it was, an old sweater, soggy and soiled.

Josie wrung water from one of the sleeves. As she did, she noticed the pockets on the front. She reached into one. Nothing. She searched the other.

To her disappointment, it was empty too. "I wonder who it belongs to," she said.

"Never mind the sweater," said Ethan. "Who does the boat belong to?"

Grandpa looked from the sweater to the boat. His face broke into a grin. "I'll bet I know," he said. He circled to the other side of the boat. "Yes, siree, just as I thought," he declared. "See this?"

A series of letters was tacked to the side of the boat. But reading the name was like solving a puzzle because some of the letters were missing. There was THE and then an O followed by a gap, then a YS and a longer gap with a Y at the end.

"I can't figure it out," said Josie.

Claire shook her head. "Me either."

Ethan shrugged. "Do you know what it says, Grandpa?"

"*The Odyssey*," Grandpa answered. "It's the only boat I know of with a name like that and it belongs to my old friend Finn MacCabe."

"*The Odyssey*?" Josie said, curious.

"That's a weird name. What does it mean?"

"Long ago there lived a man named Odysseus," said Grandpa. A look they all knew crossed his face. It meant that a story was coming.

Grandpa took off his backpack and pulled out the thermos of hot chocolate. He poured a cup for Claire and one for Ethan. Then out came the thermos of tea. He unscrewed two cups from the top, handed them to Josie and poured the hot, fragrant tea.

Neither Ethan nor Claire would touch tea. Secretly Josie didn't like the taste either, but she loved the smell and the warmth of the cup in her hands. Best of all, she liked sharing it with Grandpa.

"Odysseus sailed the ancient world for ten years," Grandpa began. "He had some fantastic adventures."

Josie's eyes widened when she heard *ancient world*. "Was that when dinosaurs were alive?" she asked.

Grandpa shook his head. "No, Jo-girl, but it was a very long time ago."

Ethan licked hot chocolate from his

lips. "Why did Finn name his boat for someone who lived way back then?"

"Ever since Finn was a kid, he dreamed of sailing around the world," Grandpa replied. "He's a man of adventure, like Odysseus."

"Did Finn sail around the world?" Claire asked.

"Not quite," said Grandpa. "But he sailed up and down the Atlantic coast. He had some amazing adventures and he has some great stories to tell." Grandpa looked at Ethan. "He's a woodcarver too."

Ethan's eyes lit up. Carving was one of his hobbies.

"Uh, oh," Claire interrupted, pointing out to sea. "Storm's coming!"

Sure enough, dark clouds were rolling in and the wind had picked up.

Grandpa hurriedly collected the cups and thermoses. "What say we drive out to Driftwood Bay and pay Finn a visit?" he suggested, taking a plastic bag from his backpack. "We can return his sweater and tell him where his boat is. You can bet he'll be looking for it."

Grandpa noticed Josie's disappointed look. "I guarantee you'll enjoy meeting Finn," he said. "He's a fascinating fellow."

"Do we have to go now?" Josie asked.

Grandpa glanced at the sky. "The rain's not going to hold off much longer."

Josie still wasn't ready to give in. "I vote we keep on fossil hunting."

"In the rain?" said Ethan. He stood up. "The fossils will still be here tomorrow," he said. "I want to see those carvings."

Claire scrambled to her feet. "It's getting colder." She shivered. "I vote we go meet Finn MacCabe."

"Looks like you're out-voted," Ethan told Josie.

Josie didn't have a choice. The McCrimmon rule was that the majority rules. Reluctantly she picked up her backpack. Meeting Finn MacCabe might be interesting, but it couldn't be as interesting as fossil hunting.

"We'd better get a move on," Grandpa urged. "Looks like we're in for a downpour."

As if the heavens had heard him, large drops splattered down on them. Fiddlehead Cove offered no shelter from the storm.

They hurried along the beach as fast as the rocks would allow. When they reached the far side of Stone Trees Point, Josie slowed for a moment and looked ahead. There was no sign of the large white dog. And no sign of Lucan. She breathed a sigh of relief.

"Hurry up," Claire called back to her. "We're getting soaked."

Josie scrambled to catch up with her sister. A little rain was okay, but this downpour was too much. Maybe putting off fossil hunting until tomorrow wasn't such a bad idea after all.

Meeting Finn MacCabe

As soon as they reached the cottage, everyone changed into dry clothes. By the time they were ready to go, the rain had faired off.

Ethan yanked the van door open and claimed the front seat. Josie and Claire scrambled into the back. Grandpa turned onto Old Beach Road and headed back the way they had come that morning.

This time they drove past the main road and followed the coast. The strip of land between the road and shore grew wider and the ocean more distant. Rain came heavy, then light, as though it couldn't make up its mind.

"I've got a riddle," Ethan said. "Why do gorillas have big nostrils?"

"I won't even hazard a guess," Grandpa replied.

Claire shook her head.

"Tell us," said Josie.

"Because they have big fingers," said Ethan.

"Yuck!" Claire made a gagging sound. Grandpa thought of another riddle and that started a round of them.

Claire had just asked, "What lies at the bottom of the ocean and twitches?" when Josie shouted out, "Driftwood Bay!"

"Wrong," Claire teased. "It's a nervous wreck."

Josie rolled her eyes. "I was reading the sign." She tapped on the window. "Grandpa said Finn lives in Driftwood Bay."

"We're almost there," Grandpa said as he turned onto a gravel road. And a bit farther on, "There's Finn's place."

Josie stared at the tidy green-and-white clapboard house. It didn't look like the kind of house a man who'd sailed the ocean and had all kinds of adventures would live in. Grandpa parked the van next to a pile of lobster traps. The doors slid open and Ethan and Claire climbed out. Josie grabbed the bag with Finn's sweater and scrambled after them.

When they reached the porch, the first thing Josie noticed was the brightly polished brass doorknocker. It was shaped like an ancient sailing ship. This is more like it, she thought.

Grandpa rapped the knocker. A voice boomed out, "Coming!" and a moment later the door swung open.

Before them stood a man with a round, weather-beaten face split right across the middle by a wide, glad-to-see-you smile. At the sight of Grandpa, his eyes lit up.

"Jake McCrimmon, you old rascal! I haven't seen you in a donkey's age." Finn clasped Grandpa's hand in a firm shake. His gaze shifted to Josie, Claire and Ethan. "And these are your grandkids, I'll bet."

Grandpa nodded, all smiles himself, and introduced them.

Finn shook hands all around. When he came to Josie, he said, "The last time I saw you, you were hardly bigger than a newborn pup. I sang you a lullaby and rocked you to sleep. I'll bet you don't remember that."

Josie's face grew hot. Why did people always have to remind her that she was the youngest?

Before she could say a word, a large black cat darted between Finn's legs onto the porch. He looked around as if to say, "Whom will I choose?" Then he headed for Josie and rolled over at her feet, exposing a snow-white belly. Josie knelt and patted him. He rewarded her with a deep, rumbling purr. Why couldn't dogs be this quiet and gentle? she wondered.

"What's his name?" she asked, looking up at Finn.

"That's Aggie," Finn replied. "Friendliest cat you'd ever want to meet." He stopped and stared as the sweater began to slip out of the bag she was still holding.

Josie caught it and passed it to Finn. "It's yours," she said.

Finn's bushy gray eyebrows shot up to his hairline. "Where did you find it?"

Ethan jumped in and told Finn how he'd found *The Odyssey*. Josie let him tell his part of the story, but she finished with, "Fiddlehead Cove's down the shore a ways, past Grandpa's cottage."

"The boat's safe and sound," Grandpa added. Josie thought her eyes would pop out of her head when Finn danced a jig right there on the porch.

"Thanks be to all of you!" he whooped. "This is one glorious day. First, my old friend Jake shows up on my doorstep. Then his grandkids tell me they've found my boat." He looked at Josie. "And thank you, little lady, for bringing back my sweater."

Little again. Josie groaned inwardly, then shivered as a gust of wind blew sharp and cold.

"Look at this!" Finn's voice boomed. "Here we're standing outside on the doorstep when inside's warm as toast.

Come make yourselves at home."

As Grandpa, Ethan and Claire followed Finn through the door, Josie looked over her shoulder to see if Aggie was coming too, but he padded regally down the steps, heading off on business of his own.

Josie caught up with the others in the front hall. Finn led them into a large room where a fire blazed a warm welcome.

As they entered, Josie stopped and stared. Claire gasped. "Wow!" Ethan exclaimed.

Next to Stone Trees Cottage, Josie decided, this was the most interesting place she'd ever seen.

Woodcarvings were everywhere. Loons, gulls, gannets, puffins, whales and dolphins. And boats. Fishing boats, sailboats, even a ferry complete with cars and passengers. Scattered among the carvings were shells of every description. Fishnets hung on the walls. Firelight reflected off the colorful glass floats that hung in the window.

"Sit right down and put your feet

up," Finn invited. "Or look around and explore. My house is your house. I'm going to heat up some cider."

Who could sit when there were so many fascinating things to see? Ethan headed for the carvings. Claire went from one table to the next, examining the shells. Josie didn't know what to look at first.

"You picked a good day to come," Finn called from the kitchen. "Alma Luther brought over one of her blueberry grunt desserts. Alma makes the best blueberry grunt in Prince Edward County."

"Can I give you a hand?" Grandpa asked, heading for the kitchen.

Ethan picked up a pair of carved seagulls standing on a piece of driftwood. "Their legs are no bigger than toothpicks," he said. "You can practically count their tail feathers!"

Claire held a large pink shell to her ear. "I've never found anything like this around here," she said.

Ethan looked at Josie. "Some place, eh?"

Josie nodded, dazzled. Then her gaze fell on an object sitting on the shelf above the fireplace. It was a skull. Before she could point it out to Claire and Ethan, Finn came back into the room, carrying a tray with steaming mugs and a stack of plates and forks. He set the tray on a table by the fireplace, the only surface in the room that wasn't crowded with treasures of one sort or another. Grandpa came behind with a large glass dish.

"Come and get it, folks," Finn said. He cut generous servings of the blueberry grunt and passed them around.

Josie was all set to ask about the skull, but Ethan spoke up first. He wanted to know about the carvings. Then Claire jumped in with questions about the shells.

Finn was so busy talking that he scarcely touched his dessert. He took time answering each question, and stories went along with most of them.

For a while Josie was content to eat and listen. The blueberry grunt was every bit as delicious as Finn said it

would be. But her eyes kept drifting back to the skull. She wiggled in her chair, impatient to ask her own questions. Finally Finn turned to her.

"Now, little lady," he said, following her gaze, "what's caught your eye?"

"The skull," Josie said. "Where did it come from?"

Finn chuckled. "That's one of my favorite stories. It happened a long time ago, back when I was a boy. It's a true story too, about a cave, a treasure and a lucky penny."

What Finn Found

"One day my buddies and I were arguing about what to do," Finn began. "Rilla and Butch wanted to go clam digging. But Al and I wanted to explore." Finn looked from one to the other. "So I took out my lucky penny, a big old copper coin my dad had brought back from England. My buddies and I settled lots of arguments with a flip of that penny," he added.

"The penny came up tails, the way Al and I'd called it. So we set off to explore around Split Cape. We'd heard there'd been a rockslide there that spring and we wanted to check it out. We poked through the rubble and what do you think we found?"

Josie, Ethan and Claire waited eagerly.

"Pieces of bone. Chunks of bone so old they'd turned to stone," said Finn. "But that's not all we found. Rilla and Butch wandered on down the beach. All of a sudden, we heard them yell, 'Come see this!'

"Al and I took off like greased lightning. When we caught up with them, they were standing at the bottom of the cliffs, looking up at something."

"What?" Josie burst in.

"A ledge, maybe two, three meters off the ground," replied Finn. "Above it was an opening. The opening looked just big enough for a kid to fit through." He paused for a sip of cider. "We scrambled up to that ledge like a pack of hungry dogs heading for dinner. There was just enough room for us to squeeze between the rocks and that's when we found it."

"What?" gasped Claire.

"A cave," said Finn.

"Wow!" Ethan drew out the word.

"Lucky!" Josie exclaimed.

"We'd been to Split Cape before, but we'd never noticed the cave. So we figured it had probably been covered up by a rockslide long ago. And the rockslide that spring had opened it up again." Finn shifted in his chair. "There was enough light coming into the cave so's we could move around and have a look-see. What we found was a cave within a cave."

"A cave within a cave?" Ethan repeated.

Finn nodded. "At the back of the cave we were standing in was another one, more just an opening really. Wide, but less than a foot high. We looked in and what do you think we saw?"

"The skull?" Josie guessed.

Finn shook his head. "Not right away. It was dark and all we could see were chunks and pieces of rock. Nothing interesting. Then we got arguing about whether to go clam digging or stay and explore some more. So what do you think I did?"

"You took out your lucky penny," Josie guessed.

"Hats off to the little lady," Finn exclaimed. "That's exactly what I did. I took out my lucky penny and flipped it." His hands did the motions. "But when I reached out to catch it ..." He let his hand drop.

"You missed!" Ethan jumped in.

Finn gave a quick nod. "It rolled right into that small cave," he said. "I wasn't about to lose my lucky penny, so I got down on my hands and knees to look. Speaking of luck, Al had some matches in his pocket. With the help of the extra light, I found my penny."

In her mind, Josie could see it all happening.

"But that's not all I found." Finn lowered his voice. "I saw something else, something white, partly embedded in a large chunk of rock."

Finn's voice rose back to normal. "When I pulled it out, what do you think I had in my hand?" Before anyone could answer, he jumped to his feet, reached up and grabbed the skull.

Claire and Josie let out a gasp.

"Of course it didn't look like this at the time. Just the top and the eye sockets were showing. The rest was still buried in the rock."

Ethan reached for the skull and examined it before passing it to Claire, who quickly passed it to Josie. She cradled it in her hands. "What's it from?" she asked.

"A Trithelodont," Finn answered.

"A Tri-th-low ..." Josie tried the word.

"Trithelodont," Grandpa spoke up. "A reptile about the size of a cat."

Finn nodded. "At the time, we didn't know what we'd really found. I took the skull home as a souvenir."

Josie ran her fingers over the surface. Imagine finding something like this! "How did you find out it's from a Trithelodont?" she asked, pleased at managing the word.

"One summer I was driving a tour boat and I got talking to a professor who lectured at Dalhousie University. He was a paleontologist, so I told him about the skull. He insisted on coming to see it that very day.

"When I showed it to him, he got so excited he could hardly talk. I let him take it back to his lab. When the surrounding rock was removed, he was able to identify the skull. Said it belonged to a Trithelodont. Said that would make it about two hundred million years old, give or take a millennium or two," Finn added with a chuckle.

"That was some find!" said Ethan.

"So the skull was the treasure," Josie declared.

"Yup," Finn said. "It even made the newspapers. I can tell you, I was some proud of that."

He went over to the shelves and took out a large book. It was filled with newspaper clippings. The first sentence of one article caught Josie's eye. "'Finn MacCabe,'" she read aloud, "'is a man who wears many hats.'" She looked at Finn. "Do you collect hats too?"

Finn shook his head. "That's just an expression, little lady. It means someone who has a lot of different interests."

"Finn's a fisherman, traveler, tour guide, woodcarver and shell collector," said Grandpa. "That's a lot of different hats, so to speak."

Josie liked the expression. I'll remember that one, she promised herself. "So this is the skull you found that day," she said, holding it carefully.

"Actually, that's a replica," said Finn. "Right now, the original skull is part of a scientific study taking place at the Smithsonian Institute in Washington."

Josie's eyes popped. Imagine. Just imagine!

"Did you ever find any more skulls?" Claire asked.

Finn shook his head. "No, but since then scientists have found lots of interesting fossils near Split Cape. Around here, I leave the fossil hunting to Jake. Your grandpa's made some great finds."

Josie gave Grandpa a proud look. He winked at her and stood up. "It's time we were going, Finn," he said. "We're having a barbecue on the beach tonight." He put a hand on Ethan's shoulder and Claire's. "These two are off to Montreal on Monday."

Finn looked at Josie. "Are you going too?"

Josie shook her head. "I'm staying at the cottage with Grandpa," she said.

Finn grinned. "You don't look too sad about that."

"I'm not." Josie grinned back. "Grandpa and I are going to have the best fun of all. We're going fossil hunting and beachcombing every single day."

Finn glanced out the window. "Looks like you're in luck for your barbecue. The rain's stopped and the sky's clearing some."

"Thanks for everything, Finn," Grandpa said at the door. "It's been a great afternoon."

"A really great afternoon," Claire echoed. "I like your shells."

"And your woodcarvings," Ethan added.

"The skull and the stories were the best of all," said Josie.

"The pleasure was mine," Finn assured them. "It's the least I could do after you found my boat and brought back my sweater." As he opened the door to let them out, Aggie jumped off the porch swing where he'd been sleeping. "Come on, Agamemnon, let's see about supper," said Finn. The cat streaked past them and disappeared inside.

"Agamemnon?" Josie said the name carefully. "Where did he get a name like that?"

"That's another story," said Finn.

"For next time," said Grandpa.

"For next time," Finn promised. "Come again," he called after them.

"We will for sure," said Josie.

The rain held off as Finn predicted, so they had their barbecue and bonfire on the beach. Later Josie fell asleep with the memory of flames shooting high into the sky and the smell of roasting hot dogs and marshmallows, gooey and dripping, toasted golden brown.

Late in the night she woke, shivering. The quilt had slipped onto the floor. She got up and wrapped it around herself. Then she tiptoed to the window, pulled back the blind and looked out at the beach.

The moon cast eerie shadows among the rocks. What was that, crouched on the sand? Her heart jumped. Stop it, she told herself, it's just a big rock. That dog's in his house. The beach is like always, safe as safe can be.

She climbed back into bed and snuggled down, yawning hugely. While she waited for sleep to come, her mind strung together bits of thought. Finn's boat ... his stories ... the rockslide ... the long-forgotten cave. And the skull ... the skull that was over two hundred million years old. Imagine finding something like that!

The Accident

Josie woke and stretched. In the next bed, Claire slept soundly. The room was dark, except for a faint edge of light peeking around the window blind.

From the kitchen came the sound of running water, then the clatter of silverware. Grandpa was up. Josie slipped out of bed and into her clothes. She tiptoed to the door and eased it open. A wonderful smell tickled her nose. Blueberry muffins!

She looked through the living room into the kitchen. Grandpa was sitting at the table with his back to her. Josie moved silently on her sock feet. Just before she reached his chair, a loose floorboard creaked. Grandpa turned. "Gotcha!" they said, at the same time.

"Good morning, Grandpa." Josie gave him a hug.

"Sleep well?" Grandpa asked, hugging her back.

"Like a log," Josie answered. She slid onto the chair across from him. A steaming mug of tea sat at Grandpa's elbow. Beside the mug was a half-eaten muffin, butter melting in the middle.

"Those blueberry muffins were calling my name, Jo-girl." Grandpa poured a glass of orange juice and set it in front of her. "We're the only two up so far. Dig in," he said, reaching her a basket piled high with muffins.

Josie helped herself to a fat one studded with blueberries. She gulped down her juice and gave her mouth a backhanded swipe. "When can we go fossil hunting?" she asked.

Grandpa glanced out the window. "The weather's not very promising. I think we're in for more rain."

Josie turned and looked. Dark clouds moved across the sky. There wasn't a ray of sun to be seen. She chewed her muffin, hardly tasting it. Yesterday, rain had ended the fossil hunt before they really got started. Was it going to ruin it again today? She looked back at the window. Wait a minute. It wasn't raining yet. "Grandpa, let's go right now," she said.

Grandpa chuckled. "Right now? Before I've had my second cup of tea?"

Josie jumped up and grabbed a thermos from the drain board. "It's the perfect time to go. Later on the tide will be in so there won't be as much beach to explore. Please, Grandpa? Let's go before the rain starts." And before Lucan and his uncle get out there with that dog, she thought.

"What about Ethan and Claire?" Grandpa reminded her.

"If we wait for them to get up, it'll start raining and we won't get to go at all," she said. "That's why we should go now."

"Bill said he'd drop by this morning," Grandpa said. He gathered up their dishes and put them in the sink. "He's planning to come with us."

Josie thought for a moment. "We'll leave a note," she said. "They can catch up with us later."

Grandpa turned from the sink. "Good idea, Jo-girl," he said. "You get the note written while I rinse the dishes."

Josie searched through the junk drawer until she found paper and a pencil.

"Dear Claire, Ethan and Dr. Larsen," she wrote. "Grandpa and I are fossil hunting near Fiddlehead Cove. You can meet us there." She signed it with a smiley face and propped the note against the muffin basket where they'd be sure to see it. Then she shrugged into her winter jacket and picked up her backpack. "Ready, Grandpa?" she asked.

"I'll make a thermos of tea and be there in two shakes of a billy goat's tail," said Grandpa.

Josie started out onto the deck. She almost shouted over her shoulder, "Hurry!" but caught herself in time.

Ethan, Claire and Dr. Larsen could join them later, but for now she wanted to go fossil hunting just with Grandpa, the way they usually did.

Outside, Josie hitched herself up onto the deck railing. She peered into the gray morning mist, looking ahead at the wide rocky beach. In the distance, the giant cliffs humped along the shore like great hulking beasts. Not a person in sight. The beach and whatever treasures it held were theirs.

"Secrets ..." Josie whispered the word. "Dinosaur secrets hidden in stone." Hurry, Grandpa, hurry, she urged silently. Grandpa said he'd be ready in two shakes of a billy goat's tail. Josie blew out a sigh. It must be a very slow billy goat. Sometimes Grandpa took forever. How could anyone dawdle when there were who-knows-what-wonders out there waiting to be found? A gust of wind blew, tossing her hair and tickling her cheeks. Josie could have sworn it was pushing her toward the beach.

Grandpa's shadow appeared in the doorway and Josie hopped off the railing.

"Those two sleepyheads are still at it," he said, stepping onto the deck. He looked up the road. "No sign of Bill yet, eh? Guess we'll just go ahead on our own, Jo-girl."

Josie raced down the steps with Grandpa right behind her. "Which way?" he asked.

"To Fiddlehead Cove," Josie said. "When we were there yesterday, I saw some new slabs of rock just beyond it. They must have broken away from the cliff since the last time we were there. It's right near where Ethan found the little bone." She looked at Grandpa. "I think we should check it out."

Grandpa nodded and Josie could see that he was pleased. "You're thinking like a true paleontologist," he said. A bubble of happiness swelled inside her. When Grandpa called her a paleontologist, she knew that he really meant it.

About halfway to the cove, a light rain began to fall. Josie pulled up her hood and Grandpa zipped his jacket, but neither one suggested turning back.

Josie kept her eyes glued to the ground. All kinds of debris had washed up on the beach. She spotted plastic bottles, bits of rope and an old shoe. Part of a net lay crumpled on the sand. Seaweed, like the hair from some mythical monster, twined around the rocks.

Grandpa stooped to examine something. Josie crouched beside him. "Anything interesting?" she asked. Grandpa picked up a rock, turned it over and shook his head. "Not this time."

Josie liked the way Grandpa said that. "Not this time" was as good as saying "maybe next time."

The earth holds many secrets, Grandpa often said. Looking with your eyes is good, but you have to look with your hands too. You have to root around and look into things and under things because the earth likes to hide its secrets. Sometimes you have to pry those secrets out. Other times they're right there waiting for you to find them.

Soon they rounded Stone Trees Point. As they neared Fiddlehead Cove, Josie could see the slanty slabs she'd noticed the day before. Beyond that, a narrow overhang bulged from the cliff wall. Below the overhang, the wall curved inward, creating a cave-like opening, protected by rock on three sides. It reminded her of Finn's story.

"Grandpa," she said, "do you think it would help if I had a lucky penny like Finn does?"

Grandpa looked at Josie. He rubbed his chin. Then he shook his head. "I don't think so, Jo-girl. Sharp eyes ..."

"... and a keen mind are what counts," Josie finished. She stopped in surprise. "*The Odyssey*'s gone!"

"Finn called last night after you went to bed," Grandpa said. "He told me he and his son would be by to get her this morning. Guess they've already come and gone."

A sudden rumbling made Josie look up. Overhead the sky had darkened. An icy rain began, then fell faster and heavier.

"Whoooee! We'd best take shelter till this blows over," Grandpa said. He and Josie hurried toward the overhang.

There was enough room for both of them to crouch beneath it. Grandpa slid his backpack from his shoulders and took out the thermos. He handed two cups to Josie and screwed off the top.

Josie held the cups while Grandpa poured the strong, hot tea. He reached for one of the cups and clinked it against Josie's. "Bottoms up," he said.

"Bottoms up," Josie repeated. She took a sip and wrinkled her nose. "I don't like the taste so much," she said, wrapping her hands around the cup. "But I like the smell and the warm."

While Grandpa drank his tea, Josie's eyes explored the upright slabs. There were three of them leaning against the cliff, wedged at the bottom by large rocks. A space between the first two slabs looked just wide enough for someone small to crawl inside. Josie was intrigued. What a neat hideout! Curiosity pulled her toward it. "I'm going to have a look-see," she said.

"Be careful, Jo-girl," said Grandpa. "The rocks are slippery today."

"I'll be careful," Josie promised. She squeezed behind the slanty slabs. Enough light came in so that she could see quite well. When she peeked out, she could see Grandpa, but she'd bet he couldn't see her. It was the perfect hideout, protected from the wind and rain.

Josie examined the newly exposed rock face. Low down there was a small cave-like crevice between the rocks. As she crouched on her knees to examine it, she put her hand on the rock beneath her for balance. Suddenly her hand slipped and she found herself wrist-deep in icy water. Josie gasped and yanked her hand back. By her feet was a small tidal pool. Seawater had collected in a hollow in the slab that lay flat on the ground beneath the upright ones.

Josie looked more closely. Pieces of broken rock were scattered over the bottom of the pool. Her eyes were drawn to one of them. She scooped it out. What she saw made her gasp in amazed delight.

On the rock were tiny raised prints. They looked like ... Josie held her breath. But could they be? Her eyes jumped back to the crystal clear water. There were more prints on the rocky bottom of the pool.

Josie reached out. Just as her fingers touched the icy water for the third time, an ominous clatter of rock crashing against rock made her jump. The crash was followed by an agonizing groan.

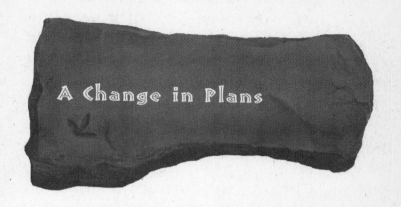

A Change in Plans

Josie dropped the piece of rock she was holding and scrambled out from behind the slabs. What she saw dashed all thought of the prints from her mind.

Grandpa was sprawled on a pile of rocks, his face tight with pain. Only one leg was visible. The other was wedged between the rocks.

Josie raced to his side. "What happened?" she cried.

"I've hurt my ankle, Jo-girl." Grandpa grimaced. "I climbed up on these rocks for a closer look at the cliff." He moved and let out a gasp of pain. "I should have known they might slide."

Josie picked and pulled at the rocks, flinging loose ones helter-skelter out of the way. Now she could see that Grandpa's ankle was firmly wedged between two large rocks. When he tried to pull his leg out, the effort brought more gasps of pain. Josie tugged at the large rocks, but they wouldn't budge.

Grandpa grabbed her arm. "Jo-girl, listen to me. We can't move these rocks by ourselves. You've got to get help. Bill may be at the cottage by now. If not, you'll have to get Jim Dunham."

Josie gulped. Get Jim Dunham? What if Hunter was on the loose again?

"Go now, Jo-girl," Grandpa said urgently.

Josie pushed herself to her feet. If she had to, she'd go to the Dunhams'. Even if it meant facing Hunter. "Don't worry, Grandpa. I'll get help," she promised. She turned and sped toward Stone Trees Point.

"Be careful, Jo-girl," Grandpa shouted after her. "We don't want any more accidents."

"Please let Grandpa be okay," Josie

said over and over as she ran through the rain, slipping and sliding, barely managing to stay on her feet.

She rounded the point. In the distance was Stone Trees Cottage. Josie peered through the rain. Was it? Oh, please let it be! Yes! Someone was standing on the deck. She charged forward, waving her arms and yelling. By now she was gasping for breath. She had a stitch in her side, and just when she thought nothing else could go wrong, she tripped and fell.

As she picked herself up, the person on the deck ran down the steps and hurried toward her. "Are you okay, Little One? What's the matter?"

Josie didn't even notice the hated name. Never in her life had she been so glad to see anyone.

"You've got to come help!" She cried. "Grandpa's hurt. His ankle's stuck. I can't move the rocks by myself."

"I'll get my first aid kit from the truck," said Dr. Larsen. "Tell me exactly where Jake is."

"Around the point." Josie gulped

back tears. "Just past Fiddlehead Cove near the overhang."

Dr. Larsen nodded. "I'll go to him. Ethan and Claire are eating breakfast. You go get them. And bring a blanket," he flung over his shoulder.

Josie raced up the slope, then took the steps to the cottage two at a time. "Grandpa's hurt!" she gasped as she burst through the door.

Claire jumped to her feet. "What happened?"

"He fell. Dr. Larsen's gone to help." Josie tried to catch her breath. "You've got to come too."

Ethan snatched his jacket as he ran to the door. "Is he okay? Where's he hurt?"

"It's his ankle." Josie grabbed a blanket and hurried after Ethan with Claire at her heels.

"Which way?" Ethan demanded at the bottom of the steps.

"Fiddlehead Cove," Josie answered and off they raced through the rain. On the way, Josie told them what had happened.

"But how did Grandpa fall?" Ethan

asked. "He's so careful on the rocks."

"I don't know," Josie said. "I didn't see it happen."

"Where were you?" Claire asked.

"I was looking at something." The little prints on the rock at the bottom of the pool flashed across her mind. Josie stopped, stunned. She'd forgotten all about them.

"What were you looking at?" Claire asked. "Come on, Josie, keep going."

Josie's feet ran as her mind whirled. The prints on the bottom of the pool! She hadn't gotten a really good look at them. Were they even prints at all? Or just natural bumps in the rock? No, she was sure they were more than that. Like prints made by a dinosaur. A very *little* dinosaur.

"So what were you looking at?" Claire persisted.

"I found some ..." Josie stopped midsentence. She was not going to say a word about those prints. Not until she'd had a chance to examine them. Not until she knew for sure what they were. And then the first person she would share them with was Grandpa. To Claire she said, "Just some little fossils. Nothing much. Come on, we've got to get to Grandpa."

When they reached the site of the accident, they found Grandpa sitting on a large rock. The foot that had been buried was propped in front of him. Dr. Larsen was wrapping a bandage around it. Josie groaned. Blood seeped through the bandage. She could see cuts and scrapes below it.

Ethan scrambled to his side. "Grandpa, are you okay?"

"Is your ankle broken?" Claire asked.

Grandpa shook his head. "I don't think so, but it's sore." Josie hugged Grandpa and wrapped the blanket around him.

"I'm sure the ankle isn't broken," Dr. Larsen agreed. "I think it's just sprained and cut. But we'd better go to the hospital and have it X-rayed."

Ethan stared at the rocky beach. "How are we going to get Grandpa back to the cottage?"

"With you on one side of him and me on the other," said Dr. Larsen.

"Between us, we'll get Jake back to the cottage. Then we'll take him to the hospital in my truck."

It was a slow, wet journey back to the cottage, but Grandpa made it. Dr. Larsen called Josie's parents. Mr. and Mrs. McCrimmon were waiting for them when they arrived at the hospital.

While X-rays were being taken, Josie told everyone what had happened. She had just finished when the doctor came out, followed by Grandpa on crutches.

"The good news is that the ankle isn't broken," the doctor said. "But it is sprained. I've taped it and he'll have to stay off it as much as possible to give it a chance to heal."

Josie's mom watched Grandpa trying to get used to the crutches. "Jake, you're coming home with us," she said.

"Definitely," Josie's dad added. "A couple of weeks of pampering is just what you need."

Josie's heart sank. No spring break at the cottage?

"But we're going to Montreal tomorrow," Ethan reminded them.

His mom shook her head. "We'll cancel the trip," she said.

Before anyone could say another word, Grandpa spoke up. "You are not going to cancel your trip for me. I can manage just fine with Jo-girl. She'll give me all the pampering I need." He winked at Josie. "What do you say? Do you still want to spend spring break at Stone Trees?"

"Yes!" Josie said. "Yes! Yes! Yes!" She turned to her parents. "I can look after Grandpa. I can cook and wash dishes and everything."

"All this fuss over a sprained ankle!" Grandpa exclaimed. "Jo-girl and I will get along just fine by ourselves."

"And I'm only a phone call away if they need anything," said Dr. Larsen.

Josie's dad looked at her mom and nodded. Ethan, Claire and Josie let out a cheer. "Let's get out of here," said Grandpa.

"Claire, Ethan, how about you two come home with us after we drive Grandpa and Josie back to the cottage?" Josie's mom suggested. "That way we can get an early start tomorrow morning."

"No need for you to drive all the way out there and back," said Dr. Larsen. "I can take Josie and Jake to the cottage. I have to go back to get my things anyway."

"We'd appreciate that, Bill," said Josie's dad. He looked at his watch. "It's past lunchtime. Is anyone hungry?" Over the chorus of yeses he said, "Let's have a bite to eat in the cafeteria."

Later, as they left the hospital, they ran into the doctor again. "Take care, Mr. McCrimmon," she said.

"I'll be back on my feet in no time," said Grandpa.

"It's okay to be on your feet, but look after that ankle. Keep off rough ground and absolutely no long hikes."

Josie stared at the doctor. "For how long?" she asked.

"A month, maybe longer," said the doctor.

Keep off rough ground? No long hikes? But you have to hike if you're going to go fossil hunting and beachcombing. And you have to hike if you're going to explore those strange prints behind the slanty rocks.

Josie felt as though she were on a roller coaster ride. Her heart soared to know that Grandpa's ankle wasn't broken. But it sank at the thought that they wouldn't be going fossil hunting together for a long time.

If Grandpa can't come with me, Josie decided, I will just have to go by myself.

Josie's Decision

That evening, Grandpa and Josie were too tired to watch the video they'd planned to. After a few hands of Crazy Eights they headed for bed, exhausted from the excitement of the day.

But Josie couldn't sleep. Visions of the little prints danced before her eyes. If the bumps on the rock really were footprints, what should she do? Tell Grandpa? No! She didn't want to tell Grandpa; she wanted to show him. But she couldn't get him there to show him, so she'd have to keep the secret a while longer. But how? How could she keep a secret about the littlest thing in the world when it might be the big-gest thing in the world? Hurry up, morning, Josie pleaded silently. Hurry up and get here with a sunshiny day perfect for exploring.

When morning came, it didn't bring the sunshine Josie had hoped for. She woke to the sound of rain splattering on the roof and waves pounding against the beach. In an instant she was out of bed and at the window.

An early spring storm was raging. Her heart sank to her toes. Exploring would have to wait.

Later, as she dried the breakfast dishes, she stared out the window. "Rain, rain, go away," she wished aloud. "I have to go out. I just have to!" she said urgently.

"Where do you have to go?" Grandpa asked.

Josie stacked the plates in the cupboard. "Back to the slanty rocks." When Grandpa looked puzzled she added, "Near where you hurt your ankle."

Grandpa's puzzled look turned to a frown. "Why do you want to go there, Jo-girl?"

The secret almost shot out of Josie's mouth, but she managed to hold it back. "To explore," she said.

"Jo-girl," Grandpa's voice was firm, "I do not want you going there by yourself. It's too dangerous. After this storm, the rocks will be slipperier than ever."

"But Grandpa ..." Josie protested.

"No buts about it," Grandpa broke in. "I'm not taking any chances on you getting hurt out there all by yourself."

"Grandpa, please!" Josie begged. "I have to go."

Grandpa shook his head. "There's nothing so important it can't wait." Seeing the disappointment on her face, he said, "How about we watch that video?"

Josie shot him a surprised look. "Now?" Grandpa never suggested TV during the day. He always said there were far more interesting things to do.

"On a day like this, why not?" Grandpa chuckled. "And we can make some of our famous peanut butter popcorn balls."

The movie took up the rest of the morning. By noon the popcorn balls were gone and they decided to skip lunch.

The rain, ignoring all Josie's pleas, still pelted down. Finally she stopped window gazing and settled on the sofa with her book. Grandpa was busy at the computer. Cozy and comfortable, Josie did something she loved to do, especially with B.J. Byers' books. She dreamed herself right into the story, sharing the mystery of *The Secret of Lost Island.*

A short while later, the book hit the floor and Josie sat up with a start. She had fallen asleep. Stretching, she got up and went to the window. More rain. Through the fog she could just make out the line of the beach. She was sure that the slanty rocks were calling her name.

Josie looked back at Grandpa. He was examining a large piece of fossilized bone. She knew the story of that bone. Grandpa had found it up the shore in an out-of-the-way place he had searched before but found nothing. But, he'd told Josie, something drew him back to it. One day, in a split in the rocks, a curved shape had caught his eye. It was the bone. And, wonder of wonders, as he'd continued exploring he'd found the jawbone of an early crocodile as well as tracks of lizards and salamanders.

What if Grandpa hadn't gone back to explore? Josie asked herself. Those tracks and bones might have stayed hidden forever. No one would ever have known about the creatures that had lived there so long ago.

The tiny prints behind the slanty rocks marched in front of Josie's eyes. Were they really dinosaur prints? Or just bumps on the rock? She had to know for sure. She had to!

As she stared at the gloomy sky, Grandpa joined her at the window. "It's a day not fit for man or beast," he said.

"I guess," Josie agreed reluctantly. Wait. Maybe it was just the right time to go exploring, when no one else would be. She didn't mind a little rain. Or even a lot of rain.

As if Grandpa had read her mind, he said, "I hope you're not thinking of going out, Jo-girl."

She knew it was useless but she had to try. "Grandpa ..." she began.

Grandpa shook his head. "Tomorrow's another day. If it brings better weather, you're a free woman." Grandpa went back to the computer, but Josie stayed at the window. One thought cheered her. If the day was not fit for man or beast, then Lucan and Hunter wouldn't be out there either. But they would be soon enough. What had Lucan said? "I'm real good at finding out secrets. And Hunter's real good at helping me." No matter what, Josie had to find the secret behind the slanty rocks before he did.

To Josie's delight, Tuesday did bring better weather. The minute the breakfast dishes were done, she grabbed her jacket.

"I promised Mom I'd find some driftwood for her," she said. And that was just what she intended to do. But she could look for driftwood and fossil hunt at the same time, couldn't she?

"Don't go far," said Grandpa.

"I won't," Josie promised.

Outside, a pale sun was trying to push back the curtain of gray, promising a clear sky later on. The tide was out and the beach stretched on forever. There wasn't a living creature in sight, aside from some gulls circling overhead.

She was almost at Stone Trees Point when something along the top of the cliffs caught her eye, a movement, a flash of color. Josie froze, staring upward. Nothing. Then she saw it again. A face, peeking through the bushes. A face with a pair of binoculars. Someone was watching her! The face withdrew suddenly, as though it had seen her looking up.

Just before it disappeared, Josie saw a blur of red. Lucan had a red jacket. Was he following her along the top of the cliffs? Spying to see where she was going so that he could discover her secret? Josie clenched her fists in frustration. She didn't dare go to the slanty rocks now. Not with Lucan watching. And where was Hunter? Was he up there too, watching her?

Josie choked back anger and fear.

She made herself walk slowly, circling back the way she'd come, keeping her eyes on the ground. Not looking behind. Not looking up. Lucan must not know she'd seen him.

She sneaked the odd glance at the top of the cliffs. A couple of times she saw a glimpse of red. So! Lucan wasn't letting her out of his sight. Anger swallowed fear as Josie realized that she had no choice but to go back to the cottage, leaving the slanty rocks to keep their secret for a while longer.

As she came in the door, Grandpa looked up from his computer. "That was a quick jaunt," he said. He took in her glum face. "No driftwood?"

"Um ... no," Josie said, realizing that she'd forgotten all about it.

Grandpa pushed his chair back and picked up his crutches. "I've done enough work for this morning," he said. "What do you say to a game of Monopoly, Jo-girl?"

Josie never said no to a game of Monopoly. "I'll set up the board," she said.

By noon her gloomy mood was long gone and she was still the McCrimmon Monopoly champion. After lunch Grandpa asked if she'd like to help him with his computer records. "Wait and see," he promised. "It'll be fun with the two of us at it." To Josie's surprise, it was.

When they stopped for a tea break, Josie yawned. "Can't have you falling asleep on me again before dinner," said Grandpa. "You need some fresh air, Jo-girl. Why don't you go do some beachcombing? Maybe you'll find some driftwood this time."

"That's just what I was planning to do," said Josie. She snatched up her jacket and yanked the door open.

"Promise me you'll be careful," Grandpa said. And just as she was about to close the door, "Don't go beyond Stone Trees Point."

Josie turned with her hand on the doorknob. "I'll be careful, Grandpa," she said. "I'll be real careful." She closed the door behind her, dashed down the steps and on down the slope to the beach. I will be careful, she repeated to herself. But I'm sorry, Grandpa. Right now, that's all I can promise.

The only thought on Josie's mind was to get to the slanty rocks. Her feet wanted to run, but she made herself walk, stopping to examine this and that. Anyone watching her would have thought that she wasn't heading anywhere in particular. Her eyes searched the top of the cliffs, the rocks, anywhere a boy and his dog could hide. She saw nothing unusual, which didn't mean Lucan and Hunter weren't out there. But it was a chance she had to take.

She rounded Stone Trees Point and passed Fiddlehead Cove. The slanty rocks were now in sight, drawing her like a magnet. Forgetting caution, she stopped, threw her arms wide and said, "World-famous paleontologist Josie McCrimmon has made a fabulous find. In a secret place behind ..."

She stopped. A sound came, a faint clatter. She spun around. Lucan's head appeared above the very rock Grandpa had fallen on.

He gave a rude snort. "World-famous paleontologist?" On Lucan's lips the words sounded weak and mocking. He circled the rock and walked over to her. Josie's eyes searched for Hunter, but he was nowhere to be seen. "So what's this fabulous find?" Lucan demanded.

"Nothing," said Josie. "I was just pretending."

"I heard you," Lucan said. "You said 'behind something.'" He gave her a hard look. "Behind what?"

Josie stared at the overhang where she and Grandpa had taken shelter the day of his accident. She let her eyes dart from the overhang to Lucan. Lucan followed her look.

"The overhang!" he shouted. "So that's the secret place! You found something behind rocks in the overhang!" He turned triumphantly and scrambled toward it.

Yes! Josie cheered silently. She had diverted Lucan's attention from the slanty rocks. He was heading in the wrong direction.

Lucan was so intent on his search

that he forgot all about her. Josie turned back toward Stone Trees Point. Away from Lucan. Away from the slanty rocks. Again! Outrage set every nerve in her body tingling. It wasn't fair. Between stormy weather and Lucan, she was never going to get a chance to examine those little prints. Then, just as she reached Fiddlehead Cove, she heard Lucan shout, "I found something!"

Josie spun around, her heart leaping to her mouth. Lucan stood by the overhang, holding something in his hand. "It's a real neat plant fossil. You want to see?"

Josie shook her head and turned away, barely managing to stifle a cheer of relief.

"I'm going to find your secret, you know," Lucan shouted after her. "If anyone's going to get lucky and make a fabulous find around here, it'll be me!"

Trapped!

Wednesday the sun shone through the early morning mist as though it planned to stay. Today's the day, Josie told herself. She thought of a bumper sticker she'd seen on a truck. *California or bust.* For me, it's the slanty rocks or bust, she thought. The only thing standing in her way was Lucan. And Hunter.

"Not hungry, Jo-girl?" Josie looked at Grandpa and then at her plate. A half-eaten pancake looked back at her.

She shook her head. "I have too much on my mind."

A short while later, Jim Dunham dropped by to return a book. When he saw Grandpa's crutches and heard about the accident, he said that he and Lucan were on their way to town and asked if he could bring them anything.

Josie barely managed not to cheer out loud. If Mr. Dunham was going to town, Lucan would be going with him. She'd be rid of him long enough to go to the slanty rocks to explore the prints. Alone!

Josie wasted no time. She gobbled the rest of her breakfast and had the dishes done in a flash.

"I thought the storms were finally over," said Grandpa in a pretend grumble. "Now it looks like we've got a whirl-wind running through the cottage."

"I'm going exploring," Josie said, pushing her arms into her jacket.

"Be back by lunchtime, Jo-girl," said Grandpa.

"I will," Josie promised, letting the door bang shut behind her.

As she hurried toward Stone Trees Point, she felt like shouting out loud. Today the beach and all its secrets were hers.

The storms and pounding waves had washed up new gifts from the sea. A small wooden box caught Josie's eye. And an oddly shaped bottle. Could it have a message inside? She hesitated, then moved on. She had no time for beachcombing today.

Rounding Stone Trees Point, she let out a sigh of relief. No one in sight. She could see the edge of Fiddlehead Cove. Beyond were the slanty rocks. Josie broke into a run.

When she reached the slanty rocks, she stopped. Everything looked the same. The three upright slabs hadn't moved. And the opening was there, like the entrance to Aladdin's Cave, leading to whatever wonders lay beyond.

Josie squeezed between the slabs. Kneeling, she looked down into the small pool. The pieces of rock were right where she'd left them. Beside the pool was the one she had dropped just after Grandpa's accident.

Josie's hand hovered. Were the marks footprints or just natural bumps? She held her breath and picked up the rock.

On the surface were two distinct sets of raised V-shaped prints. The edge of the rock was broken. Could there be more prints? Josie moved closer to the little pool. Dampness spread across the knees of her jeans.

She peered into the crystal clear water. Yes! There were more prints on the bottom of the pool. They looked just like the ones on the rock she was holding, like the tracks a bird might make in the snow in winter.

As she reached out to touch them, she froze. Was that a sound, coming from beyond the rocks? Josie listened. It came again. Someone was shouting. Josie peeked through a space between two of the slabs and let out a gasp of surprise.

Lucan was walking up the beach, heading right for the slanty rocks! And Hunter was with him. Josie jerked her head away from the space. What was Lucan doing here? Why hadn't he gone to town with his uncle?

Josie crouched in the hideout with the rock clutched in her hand. If Lucan found her here, he might discover her secret. But this was a good hiding place. If she stayed quiet, maybe they'd walk right past her. Then she could sneak out and get away from the slanty rocks.

She peeked through the space again. Let them go by, she pleaded as they came nearer. Please, let them go right on by. Lucan wasn't even looking in her direction. But Hunter was. He strained at his leash.

Lucan gave the leash a tug. "Come on, Hunter," he said, "there's nothing there. I want to have another look at that overhang."

Josie let out a shaky sigh of relief.

But she hadn't bargained on what Lucan did next. He tied Hunter's leash to a large piece of driftwood in clear view of her hiding place. "You keep guard," she heard him say. "I'm going to do some more exploring."

Josie barely stopped herself from groaning out loud. She was trapped in her hideout! Now she had no choice but to stay where she was.

Time dragged by. Behind the rocks, Josie shivered. It was cold and her jeans and feet were wet. Every once in a while, especially when she tried to move from her cramped position, Hunter barked. That brought Lucan. "What's the matter, Hunter?" he asked one time. And another, "Quit barking! There's no one around."

Josie's stomach grumbled. It was close to lunchtime. Would Lucan and Hunter never leave?

Finally Lucan appeared with a bag in his hand. "Time to go home," he said, untying Hunter's leash. "I'm hungry." Josie almost cried out with relief, but just then Hunter strained at his leash again, barking and yelping.

"I keep telling you, there's no one around," Lucan said. Hunter knew better. He dragged Lucan along, heading right for the slanty rocks.

"What do you see, Hunter?" Josie heard him say. "What's in there?" On her knees, Josie pushed as far back against the cliff wall as she could. Behind her, her feet found the crevice.

At the same moment, Hunter's head and shoulders appeared in the opening. Josie screamed, desperately trying to push herself farther away. In her panic, she didn't notice that she'd dropped the precious rock. Was the crevice big enough to hold her? She pushed backward, feet, legs, bottom, until she could go no farther.

"Who's there?" Lucan demanded.

Josie didn't answer. Two hands grabbed either side of Hunter's collar and pulled him out of the opening. Lucan's head replaced Hunter's. He gaped at Josie. "What are you doing in here?"

Gathering every ounce of courage she could, Josie snapped back at him, "What are *you* doing here? Your uncle said you were going to town."

Lucan smirked. "Fooled you, eh? I stayed home." He backed out and a moment later ducked in again holding a flashlight. Although he squirmed and wiggled, only his head and shoulders would fit through the opening. He could not get all the way in.

He clicked on his flashlight and shone

it around. The beam fell on the rock Josie had dropped. "Whoa! What's this?" he exclaimed. Before he could react, Josie reached out and grabbed the rock.

"Give me that!" Lucan ordered, trying to wiggle in farther.

Josie pushed back quickly. Then it happened. Her left foot jammed. She tried to yank her leg forward, but it wouldn't move. Her foot was firmly caught in the crevice.

She wiggled back and forth, but her foot remained wedged as though held by a giant hand. Josie was not only trapped behind the slanty rocks, she was stuck!

Facing Hunter

"You'd better come out right now or I'll send Hunter in to drag you out!" Lucan threatened. Josie gulped. She couldn't come out even if she wanted to. If he sent Hunter in, she had no way to escape. She squirmed and struggled, frantically trying to free her foot.

It didn't take Lucan long to figure out what was wrong. "You're stuck!" he jeered, watching with obvious delight as she struggled. "You can't get out." He reached toward her. "Give me that rock and I'll help you."

"No!" Josie spat out the word. She pushed the rock into her jacket pocket and zipped it shut. It dug sharply into her stomach, but she didn't care.

"Then I'll just have to get it myself," Lucan said.

"You can't even get in here," she threw back at him.

"Maybe I can't," said Lucan, retreating, "but Hunter can."

Lucan moved so quickly that Josie scarcely had time to panic. Before she knew it, Hunter had squeezed through the opening and was standing right in front of her. Josie shut her eyes, clamped her hands over her head and waited for those sharp, gleaming teeth to sink into her skin.

Nothing happened. Not a snarl nor a growl nor a crunch of sharp teeth. Instead a soft whine sounded in her ear and a warm tongue slurped across her cold hands.

Slowly, Josie eased her hands away and raised her head. Her breath whooshed out in a frightened gasp. Hunter had crouched down so that they were practically nose to nose. His tongue swiped her cheek. It felt like a kiss.

"Hunter! What are you doing?" At the sound of Lucan's voice, Hunter's ears pricked up and his head turned. "Bring her out here," Lucan ordered. Hunter looked back at Josie and whined.

"Hunter, get out here. Now!" Lucan yelled.

Hunter turned to obey. Without thinking what she was doing, Josie acted. She grabbed onto Hunter's collar and held tight.

As Hunter lunged for the opening, the sudden pull dislodged Josie's foot. She was free! She let go of Hunter's collar and he squeezed through the opening. She scrambled after him as quickly as her cramped legs could manage.

Lucan stared, stunned. "How did you ...?" His eyes narrowed. "Give me that rock."

"No, I won't," Josie said, biting off each word.

"You'll be sorry," Lucan said. He let go of Hunter's collar. "Go get her," he ordered. "Attack!"

Josie took a few steps backward.

Then, with iron will, she forced herself to stand still although her stomach was doing somersaults and her legs felt like water.

"Attack, Hunter!" Lucan yelled. "Attack! Attack!"

Hunter walked up to Josie, tail wagging, and licked her hand.

Lucan's mouth dropped open. Maybe it was nerves or maybe exhaustion that made her do it, but Lucan looked so ridiculous, standing there with his mouth gaping, that Josie burst out laughing. Laughter gave her the courage to reach out and pat Hunter.

Lucan grabbed Hunter's collar and pulled him away. "Leave my dog alone," he ordered and snapped on Hunter's leash.

Josie started to edge away, but Lucan blocked her path. "Give me that rock," he said. "If you don't hand it over, I'll take it myself."

Everything Josie had been through to get that rock — the searching, Grandpa's accident, bad weather, Lucan, Hunter, being trapped — flashed before her eyes. If Lucan thought she was going to hand over her precious rock, he had another think coming.

The beach sloped here so that Josie, standing higher than Lucan, was exactly the same height as he was. She remembered something Grandpa once said. "Bullies are cowards when it comes right down to it." Grandpa, I hope you're right, Josie thought.

Her eyes locked on Lucan's. "I'm not going to give you the rock," she said. "So you'll have to take it." Her voice came out cool and clear, but inside she was shaking so hard she thought her bones had turned to jelly.

Lucan shifted from foot to foot.

"I'm not giving you the rock," Josie repeated. "No matter what you do. Not ever."

She looked at her watch. "It's way past lunchtime. I'm going home."

Gathering every bit of courage she possessed, Josie stepped past Lucan. As she went by, she reached out and patted Hunter. "Thanks for rescuing me," she said.

To her amazement, Lucan didn't try

to stop her. Without a backward glance she hurried along the beach as quickly as her sore foot allowed. Grandpa would be worried. But when she showed him what she'd found...

"You just wait," Lucan yelled after her. "I'm going to find something much better than you did!"

Good luck trying, Josie thought without turning around.

She had just reached Stone Trees Point when she heard a voice ahead calling her name.

"I'm here!" she shouted. As she rounded the point she almost ran into Dr. Larsen.

"I think you're in a spot of trouble, Little One," said Dr. Larsen. "I dropped by to see how you and your grandpa were doing," he went on. "Jake's worried. He was just about to call some of the neighbors to look for you. I told him I'd find you."

"I didn't mean to worry him," Josie said. Ahead was Stone Trees Cottage. Never, ever, had it looked so welcoming.

Josie put her hand on her zipped pocket and felt the outline of the precious rock. Finally, she could share her secret.

"Dr. Larsen, I have to see Grandpa right now and let him know I'm okay. And," she paused, "I have something special to show him."

Dr. Larsen grinned. "I can take a hint. You go ahead. I'll putter around out here for a bit."

"Thanks," Josie said. Ignoring her sore foot, she almost flew across the rocky beach, bringing her secret to Stone Trees Cottage and Grandpa.

A Surprise for Grandpa

When Josie opened the door, Grandpa was waiting for her. She hesitated. He knew she'd disobeyed him. What was he going to say? "Grandpa ..." she began.

"Jo-girl, I was worried about you," he broke in and opened his arms wide. Josie was in them in a second.

"Grandpa, I'm so sorry," she said. "I have to tell you ..."

He put his hands on her shoulders. "First things first," he said. "You need a hot bath and dry clothes."

"Wait, Grandpa." Josie stood firm. "I have something to show you. Something very important." She took the rock from her pocket and put it into Grandpa's hand. "This is why I went back to the slanty rocks."

Grandpa stared at the rock. He ran his fingers over the little raised prints. He blinked. "Footprints. Footprints of a little dinosaur." His eyes fixed on Josie. "Jo-girl, I believe you have found the proof we've been looking for! Where did you find them?"

Josie told him how she had discovered the footprints. When she got to the part about hiding from Lucan, Grandpa interrupted to ask, "Did that boy give you any trouble?"

"Nothing I couldn't handle," said Josie. "And I made friends with Hunter," she added. Her attention went back to the rock. "There are more footprints where I found those."

Grandpa shook his head as though he couldn't believe his eyes. "What a find!"

Feet sounded on the steps and Dr. Larsen came through the door. He glanced from Josie to Grandpa. "What's going on?" he asked.

"I found something special behind the slanty rocks," Josie said, trying to keep her voice calm.

Grandpa handed the rock to Dr. Larsen. He looked at it; then he dug into his pocket, yanked out a magnifying glass and examined the rock inch by inch. His eyes went to Josie. Back to the rock. Back to Josie. Finally, in a voice filled with awe, he asked, "Do you have any idea what you've found, Little One?"

Josie nodded. "Dinosaur tracks. Footprints from a really little dinosaur." The words spun cartwheels in her head. "Maybe the littlest dinosaur in the whole world."

"I believe you're right," said Dr. Larsen. "How about you and I go back and explore the site tomorrow morning?"

"All right!" said Josie.

"Right now, Jo-girl," Grandpa said, "you need a hot bath. Meanwhile I'll heat up the seafood chowder Bill brought over." He looked at Dr. Larsen. "Will you share a late lunch with us?"

"I'd like that," replied Dr. Larsen. "I want to hear the whole story." He winked at Josie. "Maybe while we're eating the chocolate fudge brownies I brought for dessert."

Chocolate fudge brownies? Her absolute favorite! "All right!" Josie whooped. "I'll be back in two shakes of a billy goat's tail."

She raced to the bathroom. On went the water, off came her clothes and she scrambled into the tub. Warmth wrapped around her like a soft wool blanket. Could anything be better than this? Here she was, back at the cottage, safe and sound, celebrating her fabulous find. Voices rose and fell excitedly in the next room. Grandpa and Dr. Larsen were talking about the prints.

The prints. No, Josie corrected herself. The footprints. Because that's what they were. Grandpa and Dr. Larsen had said so. Dinosaur footprints. Imagine. Just imagine! Footprints of a very little dinosaur. Maybe the littlest dinosaur in the world. And she had found them.

Josie Renee McCrimmon, paleontologist!

"Hurry up, Jo-girl," Grandpa called. "Chowder's hot, toast's buttered and those brownies are about to jump off the plate at us. Bill's waiting to hear the whole story."

Josie hopped out of the bath, dried off and dressed in her favorite cozy sweat suit. She hurried to the kitchen, slid onto her seat at the table and, once again, between mouthfuls of chowder, toast and chocolate fudge brownies, she told the story of her fabulous find.

That night Josie fell asleep as soon as her head hit the pillow. The next morning she was up early. Dr. Larsen was coming and they were going back to the slanty rocks to see the rest of the prints. If only Grandpa could come too, Josie thought. But at least she had shared her find with him first. Except for Lucan, but he didn't count.

Breakfast was porridge, not the French toast Josie had hoped for. She made a wry face, but figured that she could probably get the porridge down if she flooded it with maple syrup and milk. She was reaching for the pitcher when Grandpa said, "Jo-girl, we need to have a talk."

Josie concentrated on her porridge. She knew what was coming.

"You promised me you wouldn't go beyond Stone Trees Point," Grandpa began.

Josie swallowed. "No, I didn't, Grandpa. Not exactly."

Grandpa gave her a look and Josie went on. "I never exactly promised you I wouldn't go to the slanty rocks." Josie poured on more syrup. "I didn't promise because I had to go back. And I couldn't go with you so I had to go alone."

Grandpa's mouth opened and closed as though he didn't know what to say. "You put yourself in a lot of danger," he said finally. "You should have told me why you wanted to go back. Dr. Larsen could have gone with you."

Josie made a hollow in her porridge and watched the syrup and milk run into it. "At first I wasn't sure what I'd found," she said. "So I had to go back for a second look." Her eyes met Grandpa's. "I didn't want to share my find with anyone but you."

Grandpa smiled in spite of himself. "Promise me you'll never do anything like that again, Jo-girl."

Josie beamed. "The next time I make a fabulous find, I'll come right away and tell you," she promised.

A short while later there was a knock on the door. "I'll bet that's Dr. Larsen," Josie said, racing to answer it.

But when she opened the door, Lucan stood on the deck. "Can you come out here for a minute?" he asked.

Josie grabbed her jacket and shrugged into it. As she stepped through the door, Hunter bounded toward her. Josie backed off, still a bit unsure.

"Sit, Hunter," Lucan ordered. "Stay." He fidgeted from foot to foot. "I'm sorry about yesterday. I told my uncle about the prints you found. I thought he'd be mad because I didn't find them first. But he said he couldn't sell anything like that in his shop anyway. He said important fossils aren't meant for souvenirs."

Josie remembered how frightened she had been, trapped behind the slanty rocks with Lucan threatening her. She wasn't going to let him off that easily.

"You tried to make Hunter attack me," she said.

Lucan looked away, then back. "Actually I'm not training him to be an attack dog. I want to train him for Search and Rescue."

Josie played with the zipper of her jacket. "Someone came to my class last year and told us about that," she said, wondering if there might be a nice side to Lucan after all.

Hunter moved toward her. She patted him and he wagged his tail.

"He likes you," said Lucan. As if to confirm, Hunter jumped up and tried to lick her face. Lucan pulled him back. "Sorry," he said. "He's just a pup." He hesitated as though he had something else to say. Finally he got it out. "I guess you're going to tell my uncle what happened."

Josie's eyes narrowed. "So that's why you came to say sorry. You're afraid

I'll tell your uncle."

"Sort of," said Lucan. "My uncle warned me to leave you alone. Now he might take Hunter away." He knelt and hugged Hunter. "But that's not the only reason ..." He hesitated again and his cheeks went red. "You were real brave."

"I can fight my own battles," Josie said stiffly. "Anyway, I wasn't going to tell your uncle."

Lucan gave her a surprised look. "You mean it?"

Josie nodded.

A long moment passed. "I'd better go," Lucan said. He started down the steps then he turned. "So I'll see you around?"

"Yes you will," said Josie. She watched them head toward the road. Much to her surprise, she found herself thinking that seeing them around might not be such a bad thing after all.

Josie Leads the Way

Dr. Larsen arrived shortly after Lucan left. "Ready?" he asked when Josie opened the door.

"I sure am," said Josie. She still had her jacket on.

"I wish I were coming with you," said Grandpa, frowning at his crutches.

"I wish you were too," said Josie.

"We'll bring back lots of pictures, Jake," Dr. Larsen promised. "Now," he said to Josie, "lead me to the site of your fabulous find."

Overhead the sun shone brightly, as though it knew this was a special day. And it is, Josie marveled. Just imagine. Me, Josie Renee McCrimmon, leading the way to a fabulous find!

Soon they were back at the slanty rocks. "This is the place," Josie said, feeling pings of excitement as she hurried toward it.

Together they examined the slanty slabs. The middle one shifted a bit when Dr. Larsen put his weight on it. Not only was the slab loose, but so were the rocks that held it wedged on a slant. With a bit of a struggle, Dr. Larsen was able to move the rocks out of the way. "Stand back, Josie," he said. "I'm going to try to push this slab over."

Josie stared at him. It was the first time he'd ever called her anything but Little One.

Her attention went back to the rocks as Dr. Larsen tugged and wiggled at the slab. It teetered, then tumbled with a crash. A pair of gulls exploring a nearby tidal pool took off in fright, scolding as they went. Josie scarcely noticed them. She stared at the fallen slab. Her hideout was no more.

She crouched and peered into the

pool. "Look, Dr. Larsen. More prints, just like I said." She touched the tiny prints. "They must be from a very little dinosaur, don't you think? Maybe the littlest one in the whole world!"

Dr. Larsen nodded. "Jake and I thought that there were little dinosaurs," he said. "But knowing isn't as good as showing. You found the proof we've been looking for, Josie."

"I wish Grandpa could see this," Josie said.

"He can," said Dr. Larsen. He reached into his backpack and pulled out a camera. Josie had never seen one like it.

"It's a digital video camera," he explained. He took several pictures of the surrounding area and the slabs while he talked. Then he showed Josie the pictures he'd taken, right there on a tiny screen attached to the camera. "It records my voice too," he said. Josie was amazed.

Dr. Larsen focused on the pool and the tiny prints. He turned to Josie. "Now we want some pictures of the person who made the discovery," he said.

As he photographed Josie by the little pool, pointing to the prints, she heard him say, "This amazing discovery was made by a young paleontologist named Josie McCrimmon." The words danced in Josie's head. "Amazing discovery ... young paleontologist ..." Imagine!

Finally he shut off the camera. "Let's head back to Stone Trees Cottage," he said. "Jake will be waiting."

On the way back, Josie tried to visualize the little creature that had made the prints so long ago. "Those rocks kept their secret for a very long time," she said out loud. "Imagine keeping a secret for millions of years."

Dr. Larsen nodded. "If it hadn't been for your sharp eyes, Josie, those rocks might have kept their secret for another million years."

Friday morning Josie was up and dressed earlier than usual. She was so excited she could hardly eat a bite of breakfast.

Grandpa had called a friend of his who worked for the newspaper, and a reporter and photographer were coming to interview her. They wanted to do a feature article about her find.

Josie looked out the window for the umpteenth time.

"You're going to wear out the glass for sure," said Grandpa.

She spotted a car driving slowly along Old Beach Road. "I'll bet that's them," she said. Moments later the car turned into the driveway.

A man and a woman got out. The man had a camera hanging around his neck and the woman was carrying a notebook. Josie had the door open before they could knock.

The woman introduced herself. "I'm Sandy Langton. And this is Angus Ford," she added, nodding at the photographer. "We're from *The Valley Herald*. We're here to do a story on the person who found the dinosaur prints."

"That's me," said Josie.

"I'm very pleased to meet you," said Sandy. "What a story this is going to make! I can't wait to hear all the details." She got right down to business. At first Josie was a bit nervous. Imagine, she thought, me, Josie McCrimmon, being interviewed by someone as important as a newspaper person. But Sandy put her at ease. She wanted to hear everything Josie had to tell about finding the remarkable footprints. It all went into her notebook. Josie had never seen anyone write so fast.

Later Josie led them to the slanty rocks so Angus could take some pictures.

"The story will be in tomorrow's paper," Sandy told Josie as she and Angus got ready to leave. "This is one of the most interesting interviews I've ever done," she added. She shook Josie's hand. "I have a feeling we'll be hearing a lot more from you in the future."

The article appeared in Saturday's newspaper, just as Sandy had promised. In fact, it was right on the front page titled "Budding Paleontologist Makes a Fabulous Find."

"They didn't say where I actually

found the prints," said Josie.

"I asked them not to," said Grandpa. "If they had, there'd be people swarming the beach wanting to see for themselves."

Josie nodded. "They put in three pictures," she said. "Three!" She studied them. "I think I like the one of you and me best." She paused. "Or maybe the one of me by the slanty rocks. Or the close-up of the footprints."

"Read the article to me again, Jo-girl," said Grandpa.

This was the fourth time Josie had read the article. She'd already read it once to Grandpa and then to her parents and to Ethan and Claire, long distance to Montreal.

"I asked Sandy to send us extra copies," Grandpa said when she had finished. "I figured you'd want to paste one in your record book."

Like Finn MacCabe's scrapbook! Josie went to the drawer and dug out her old ratty, tatty green book. Another page came loose. She looked at Grandpa. "I'm going to wait till I get a new book," she said.

Grandpa's eyes twinkled. He went to his bedroom and came back with a package. "Wait no longer," he said and handed it to her.

Josie tore off the wrapping. Inside was a large book, royal blue, with a hard cover. In gold letters across the front was "RECORD BOOK." Below that, "Josie McCrimmon, Paleontologist."

It was the most beautiful book Josie had ever seen. "Oh, Grandpa, thank you!" She ran to hug him. "It's perfect."

"I've been saving it for you, Jo-girl," said Grandpa. "I figured it would come in handy someday."

Josie took a pen from a jar on the counter and sat at the kitchen table. "I'm going to record the footprints now," she said, loving the sound of the words, so grown up and full of importance.

Grandpa went into the living room. "I'll leave you to it, Jo-girl."

Josie's fingers traced the gold letters. She felt the same tingle of excitement as she had when she'd touched the raised footprints. She opened the book.

Usually the McCrimmons' record books just contained the date, what they'd found and where. Josie decided that her book would be different. She carefully cut out and glued in the newspaper article. Just like Finn MacCabe's scrapbook. Then, in her own words, she wrote the story of finding the tiny footprints. She read it over. It sounded like a chapter from one of B.J. Byers' books. Whoooee! Her beautiful blue book was now a record book, a scrapbook and a storybook!

Josie closed the book and went to the window. White clouds scudded across a bright spring sky. "I'm going beachcombing, Grandpa," she called, grabbing her jacket from the coat hook.

"Have fun," Grandpa called back.

She stood on the deck, looking out over the beach. Near Stone Trees Point, something caught her eye. It was Hunter, pacing back and forth. His leash seemed to be caught among some large rocks. Farther on, out of sight of Hunter, a person in a bright red jacket was walking along, trailing something behind him.

Lucan. But what was he trailing? And why? Josie dashed back inside and grabbed the binoculars. If Lucan could spy on her, she could spy on him too.

Now she could see clearly. Lucan was dragging an old jacket. He stopped by some rocks, took the hood off the jacket and stuffed the rest of it behind the rocks. What was he doing? Josie watched him jog back to where Hunter was waiting. Lucan let Hunter sniff the hood of the jacket; then he took off his leash.

Hunter bounded ahead, nose to the beach. He headed for the rocks where Lucan had hidden the jacket. Moments later, Hunter scrambled across the rocks and began to tug at the jacket. Lucan caught up, and Josie could see him praising Hunter.

Of course! Search and Rescue. Lucan had said he was training Hunter. Josie watched as they disappeared around Stone Trees Point.

She ran down the steps and headed up the beach. Whenever something interesting caught her eye, she stopped to examine it. A rock with strange markings. Driftwood. A piece of pale green glass, worn smooth by the sea. Josie could no more walk past them than she could rise and fly like a gull.

When I grow up, she told herself, I'm going to be a paleontologist for sure. And a beachcomber. And maybe a writer.

In the distance she heard Lucan shout and Hunter bark. She hurried to catch up with them. Who knows, someday I may even train dogs for Search and Rescue. After all, a person can wear more than one hat, can't she?

Author's Note

Millenniums-old secrets hidden in stone. Clues to the mysteries of times long ago. Answers to the puzzles of evolution and extinction. All of these can be found in plenty along Nova Scotia's Bay of Fundy coast, where fossils dating as far back as 300 to 350 *million* years have been found.

High tides along the Fundy shore, particularly in the region of Parrsboro and Joggins, have yielded some of the most important information we have about the age of dinosaurs. These powerful tides, reported to be the highest in the world, have washed away at Parrsboro's great ancient rift valley, exposing sediments and fossils that date from the very beginning of the dinosaur era. Major discoveries, including the tiny three-toed footprints of a creature about the size of a robin, have been made in this area.

At Joggins, ragged cliffs give clues to the once-fertile woodland that flourished long ago along these barren shores.

Here ancient tree trunks were found in which fossilization is so complete that the pattern of the bark can clearly be seen. This region, so rich in clues, secrets and answers, has intrigued scientists and geologists since the pioneering days of paleontology in the mid-1800s.

But the area has also attracted amateurs – men, women and children with the same passionate interest in unlocking the mysteries of the dinosaur era. Self-taught, armed with knowledge gained from books and articles, these dedicated enthusiasts trek for miles, exploring the beaches, cliffs and riverbeds. Always pushing them onwards is the dream of making that fabulous find, that remarkable discovery. And sometimes, that is exactly what happens ...

MH

Marilyn Helmer has a long-standing interest in dinosaurs. Her son studied paleontology and geology in university. On holidays, the family often included fossil hunting and beachcombing in their plans. Marilyn is the author of many other books for children, including *Fog Cat* (Kids Can, 1998), winner of the I.O.D.E. Book Award and Mr. Christie's Book Award. She lives in Burlington, Ontario, with her husband, Gary, and her cat, Misty.

More Orca Young Readers:

Dog Days (Citra)
Danger at the Landings (Citra)
Flight from Big Tangle (Daher)
The Freezing Moon (Citra)
Ellie's New Home (Citra)
The Reunion (Pearce)
Birdie for Now (Little)
Jo's Triumph (Tate)
TJ and the Haunted House (Hutchins)
TJ and the Cats (Hutchins)
Chance and the Butterfly (deVries)
Jesse's Star (Schwartz)
The Keeper and the Crows (Spalding)
Daughter of Light (attema)
Phoebe and the Gypsy (Spalding)

Basketball by Eric Walters:
Off Season
Road Trip
Long Shot
Hoop Crazy
Full Court Press
Three on Three

Free teachers' guides are available for many Orca
Young Readers.
Visit: www.orcabook.com
or call 1-800-210-5277 for your copies.